THE PURPLE HEART OF ERLIK

BY

ROBERT E. HOWARD

British Library Cataloguing-in-Publication Data
A catalogue record for this book is available from the
British Library

Robert E. Howard

Robert Ervin Howard was born in Peaster, Texas in 1906. During his youth, his family moved between a variety of Texan boomtowns, and Howard – a bookish and somewhat introverted child – was steeped in the violent myths and legends of the Old South. Although he loved reading and learning, Howard developed a distinctly Texan, hardboiled outlook on the world. He became a passionate fan of boxing, taking it up at an amateur level, and from the age of nine began to write adventure tales of semi-historical bloodshed. In 1919, when Howard was thirteen, his family moved to the Central Texas hamlet of Cross Plains, where he would stay for the rest of his life.

At fifteen Howard began to read the pulp magazines of the day, and to write more seriously. The December 1922 issue of his high school newspaper featured two of his stories, 'Golden Hope Christmas' and 'West is West'. In 1924 he sold his first piece – a short caveman tale titled 'Spear and Fang' – for $16 to the not-yet-famous *Weird Tales* magazine. He published with the magazine regularly over the next few years. 1929 was a breakout year for Howard, in that the 23-year-old writer began to sell to other magazines, such as *Ghost Stories* and *Argosy*, both of whom had previously sent him hundreds of rejection slips. In 1930, he began a correspondence with weird fiction master H. P. Lovecraft which ran up to his death six years later, and is regarded as one of the great correspondence cycles in all of fantasy literature.

It was partly due to Lovecraft's encouragement that Howard created his most famous character, Conan the Cimmerian. Conan – a barbarian-turned-King during the Hyborian Age, a mythical period of some 12,000 years ago – featured in seventeen *Weird Tales* stories between 1933 and 1936, and is now regarded as having spawned the 'sword and sorcery' genre, making Howard's influence on fantasy literature comparable to that of J. R. R. Tolkien's. The Conan stories have since been adapted many times, most famously in the series of films starring Arnold Schwarzenegger.

Howard was enjoying an all-time high in sales by the beginning of 1936, but he was also deeply upset by the ill health of his mother, who had fallen into a coma. On the morning of June 11, 1936, he asked an attending nurse whether she would ever recover, and the nurse replied negatively. Howard walked to his car, parked outside the family home in Cross Plains, and shot himself. He died eight hours later, aged just thirty.

"You'll do what I tell you—or else!" Duke Tremayne smiled cruelly as he delivered his ultimatum. Across the table from him Arline Ellis clenched her white hands in helpless rage. Duke Tremayne, world adventurer, was tall, slim, darkly mustached, handsome in a ruthless way; and many women looked on him with favor. But Arline hated him, with as good reason as she feared him.

But she ventured a flare of rebellion.

"I won't do it! It's too risky!"

"Not half as risky as defying me!" he reminded her. "I've got you by the seat of your pretty pants, my dear. How would you like to have me tell the police why you left Canton in such a hurry? Or tell them my version of that night in Baron Takayami's apartment—"

"Hush!" she begged. She was trembling as she glanced fearfully about the little curtained alcove in which they sat. It was well off the main floor of the Bordeaux Cabaret; even the music from the native orchestra came only faintly to their ears. They were alone, but the words he had just spoken were dynamite, not even safe for empty walls to hear.

"You know I didn't kill him—"

"So you say. But who'd believe you if I swore I saw you do it?"

She bent her head in defeat. This was the price she must pay for an hour of folly. In Canton she had been indiscreet enough to visit the apartments of a certain important Japanese official. It had been only the harmless escapade of a thrill-hunting girl.

She had found more thrills than she wanted, when the official had been murdered, almost before her eyes, by his servant, who she was sure was a Russian spy. The murderer had fled, and so had she, but not before she had been seen leaving the house by Duke Tremayne, a friend of the slain official. He had kept silent. But the murderer had taken important documents with him in his flight, and there was hell to pay in diplomatic circles.

It had been an international episode, that almost set the big guns of war roaring in the East. The murder and theft remained an unsolved mystery to the world at large, a wound that still rankled in the capitals of the Orient.

Arline had fled the city in a panic, realizing she could never prove her innocence, if connected with the affair. Tremayne had followed her to Shanghai and laid his cards on the table. If she did not comply with his wishes, he'd go to the police and swear he saw her murder the Jap. And she knew his testimony would send her to a firing squad, for various governments were eager for a scape-goat with which to conciliate the wrathful Nipponese.

Terrified, Arline submitted to the blackmail. And now Tremayne had told her the price of his silence. It was not what she had expected, though, from the look in his eyes

4

as he devoured her trim figure from blonde hair to French heels, she felt it would come to that eventually. But here in the Bordeaux, a shady rendezvous in the shadowy borderland between the European and the native quarters, he had set her a task that made her flesh crawl.

He had commanded her to steal the famous Heart of Erlik, the purple ruby belonging to Woon Yuen, a Chinese merchant of powerful and sinister connections.

"So many men have tried," she argued. "How can I hope to succeed? I'll be found floating in the Yangtze with my throat cut, just as they were."

"You'll succeed," he retorted. "They tried force or craft; we'll use a woman's strategy. I've learned where he keeps it— had a spy working in his employ and he learned that much. He keeps it in a wall safe that looks like a dragon's head, in the inner chamber of his antique shop, where he keeps his rarest goods, and where he never admits anybody but wealthy women collectors. He entertains them there alone, which makes it easy."

"But how am I going to steal it, with him in there with me?"

"Easy!" he snapped. "He always serves his guests tea. You watch your chance and drop this knock-out pill in his tea."

He pressed a tiny, faintly odorous sphere into her hand.

"He'll go out like a candle. Then you open the safe, take the ruby and skip. It's like taking candy from a baby. One reason I picked you for this job, you have a natural gift for unraveling Chinese puzzles. The safe doesn't have a dial. You press the dragon's teeth. In what combination, I don't know. That's for you to find out."

"But how am I going to get into the inner chamber?" she demanded.

"That's the cream of the scheme," he assured her. "Did you ever hear of Lady Elizabeth Willoughby? Well, every antique dealer in the Orient knows her by sight or reputation. She's never been to Shanghai, though, and I don't believe Woon Yuen ever saw her. That'll make it easy to fool him. She's a young English woman with exotic ideas and she spends her time wandering around the world collecting rare Oriental art treasures. She's worth millions, and she's a free spender.

"Well, you look enough like her in a general way to fit in with any description Woon Yuen's likely to have heard. You're about the same height, same color of hair and eyes, same kind of figure—" his eyes lit with admiration as they dwelt on the trim curves of bosom and hips. "And you can act, too. You can put on an English accent that would fool the Prince of Wales, and act the high-born lady to a queen's taste.

"I've seen Lady Elizabeth's cards, and before I left Canton I had one made, to match. You see I had this in mind, even then." He passed her a curious slip of paper-thin jade, carved with scrawling Chinese characters.

"Her name, of course, in Chinese. She spends a small fortune on cards like that, alone. Now go back to your apartment and change into the duds I had sent up there—scarlet silk dress, jade-green hat, slippers with ivory heels, and a jade brooch. That's the way Lady Elizabeth always dresses. Eccentric? You said it! Go to Woon Yuen's shop and tell him you want to see the ivory Bon. He keeps it in the inner chamber. When you get in there, do your stuff, but be careful! They say Woon Yuen worships that ruby, and burns incense to it. But you'll pull the wool over his eyes, all right. Be careful he doesn't fall for you! Couldn't blame him if he did."

He was leaning toward her, and his hand was on her knee. She flinched at the feel of his questing fingers. She loathed his caresses, but she dared not repulse him. He was arrogantly possessive, and she did not doubt that when—and if—she returned with the coveted gem, he would demand the ultimate surrender. And she knew she would not dare refuse him. Tears of helpless misery welled to her eyes, but he ignored them. Grudgingly he withdrew his hand and rose.

"Go out by the back way. When you get the ruby, meet me at room Number 7, in the Alley of Rats—you know the place. Shanghai will be too hot for you, and we'll have to get you out of town in a hurry. And remember, sweetheart," his voice grew hard as his predatory eyes, and his arm about her waist was more a threat than a caress, "if you double-cross me, or if you flop on this job, I'll see you stood before a Jap firing squad if it's the last thing I do. I won't accept any excuses, either. Get me?"

His fingers brushed her chin, trailed over the soft white curve of her throat, to her shoulder; and as he voiced his threat, he dug them in like talons, emphasizing his command with a brutality that made Arline bite her lip to keep from crying out with pain.

"Yes, I get you."

"All right. Get going." He spanked her lightly and pushed her toward a door opposite the curtained entrance beyond which the music blared.

The door opened into a long narrow alley that eventually reached the street. As Arline went down this alley, seething with rebellion and dismay for the task ahead of her, a man stepped from a doorway and stopped her. She eyed him suspiciously, though concealing a secret throb of admiration for a fine masculine figure.

He was big, broad-shouldered, heavy-fisted, with smoldering blue eyes and a mop of unruly black hair under a side-tilted seaman's cap. And he was Wild Bill Clanton, sailor, gun-runner, blackbirder, pearl-poacher, and fighting man de luxe.

"Will you get out of my way?" she demanded.

"Wait a minute, Kid!" He barred her way with a heavy arm, and his eyes blazed as they ran over the smooth bland curves of her blond loveliness. "Why do you always give me the shoulder? I've made it a point to run into you in a dozen ports, and you always act like I had the plague."

"You have, as far as I'm concerned," she retorted.

"You seem to think Duke Tremayne's healthy," he growled resentfully.

She flinched at the name of her master, but answered spiritedly: "What I see in Duke Tremayne's none of your business. Now let me pass!"

But instead he caught her arm in a grip that hurt.

"Damn your saucy little soul!" he ripped out, anger fighting with fierce desire in his eyes. "If I didn't want you so bad, I'd smack your ears back! What the hell! I'm as good a man as Duke Tremayne. I'm tired of your superior airs. I came to Shanghai just because I heard you were here. Now are you going to be nice, or do I have to get rough?"

"You wouldn't dare!" she exclaimed. "I'll scream—"

A big hand clapped over her mouth put a stop to that.

"Nobody interferes with anything that goes on in alleys behind dumps like the Bordeaux," he growled, imprisoning her arms and lifting her off her feet, kicking and struggling. "Any woman caught here's fair prey."

He kicked open the door through which he had reached the alley, and carried Arline into a dim hallway. Traversing this with his writhing captive, he shoved open a door that opened on it. Arline, crushed against his broad breast, felt the tumultuous pounding of his heart, and experienced a momentary thrill of vanity that she should rouse such stormy emotion in Wild Bill Clanton, whose exploits with the women of a hundred ports were as widely celebrated as his myriad bloody battles with men.

He entered a bare, cobwebby room, and set her on her feet, placing his back against the door.

"Let me out of here, you beast!" She kicked his shins vigorously.

He ignored her attack.

"Why don't you be nice?" he begged. "I don't want to be rough with you. Honest, kid, I'd be good to you—better than Tremayne probably is—"

For answer she bent her blonde head and bit his wrist viciously, even though discretion warned her it was probably the worst thing she could do.

"You little devil!" he swore, grabbing her. "That settles it!"

Scornful of her resistance he crushed her writhing figure against his chest, and kissed her red lips, her furious eyes, her flaming cheeks and white throat, until she lay panting and breathless, unable to repel the possessive arms that drew her closer and closer.

She squirmed and moaned with mingled emotions as he sank his head, eagerly as a thirsty man bending to drink, and pressed his burning lips to the tender hollow of her throat. One hand wandered lower, to her waist, locked her against him despite her struggles.

In a sort of daze she found herself on the dingy cot, with her skirt bunched about her hips. The gleam of her own white flesh, so generously exposed, brought her to her senses, out of the maze of surrender into which his strength was forcing her. Her agile mind worked swiftly. As she sank back, suddenly she shrieked convulsively.

"My back! Something's stabbed me! A knife in the mattress—"

"What the hell?" He snatched her up instantly and whirled her about, but she had her hands pressed over the small of her back, and was writhing and moaning in well-simulated pain.

"I'm sorry, kid—" he began tearing the mattress to pieces, trying to find what had hurt her, and as he turned his back, she snatched a heavy pitcher from the wash-stand and smashed it over his head.

Not even Wild Bill Clanton could stand up under a clout like that. He went down like a pole-axed ox—or bull, rather—and she darted through the door and down the hall. Behind her she heard a furious roar that lent wings to her small high heels. She sprang into the alley and ran up it, not stopping to arrange her garments.

As she emerged into the street, a backward glance showed her Clanton reeling out into the alley, streaming blood, a raging and formidable figure. But she was on a semi-respectable street, with people strolling past and Sikh policemen within call. He wouldn't dare come out of the alley after her. She walked sedately away, arranging her dress as she went. A few loungers had seen her run from the alley, but they merely smiled in quiet amusement and made no comment. It was no novelty in that quarter to see a girl run from a back alley with her breasts exposed and her skirt pulled awry.

But a few deft touches smoothed out her appearance, and a moment later, looking cool, unruffled and demure as though she had just stepped out of a beauty shop, she was headed for her apartment, where waited the garments she must don for her dangerous masquerade.

An hour later she entered the famous antique shop of Woon Yuen, which rose in the midst of a squalid native quarter like a cluster of jewels in a litter of garbage. Outside it was unpretentious, but inside, even in the main chamber with its display intended to catch the fancy of tourists and casual collectors, the shop was a colorful riot of rich artistry.

A treasure trove in jade, gold, and ivory was openly exhibited, apparently unguarded. But the inhabitants of the quarter were not fooled by appearances. Not one would dare to try to rob Woon Yuen. Arline fought down a chill of fear.

A cat-footed Chinese bowed before her, hands concealed in his wide silken sleeves. She eyed him with the languid indifference of an aristocrat, and said, with an accent any Briton would have sworn she was born with: "Tell Woon Yuen that Lady Elizabeth Willoughby wishes to see the ivory Bon." The slant eyes of the impassive Chinese widened just a trifle at the name. With an even lower bow, he took the fragment of jade with the Chinese characters, and kowtowed her into an ebony chair with dragon-claw feet, before he disappeared through the folds of a great dark velvet tapestry which curtained the back of the shop.

She sat there, glancing indifferently about her, according to her role. Lady Elizabeth would not be expected to show any interest in the trifles displayed for the general public. She believed she was being spied on through some peephole. Woon Yuen was a mysterious figure, suspected of strange activities, but so far untouchable, either by his many enemies or by the authorities. When he came, it was so silently that he was standing before her before she was aware of his entrance.

She glanced at him, masking her curiosity with the bored air of an English noblewoman.

Woon Yuen was a big man, for a Chinese, squattily built, yet above medium height. His square, lemon-tinted face was adorned with a thin wisp of drooping mustachios, and his bull-like shoulders seemed ready to split the seams of the embroidered black silk robe he wore. He had come to Shanghai from the North, and there was more Mongol than Chinese in him, as emphasized by his massive forearms, impressive even beneath his wide sleeves. He bowed, politely but not obsequiously. He seemed impressed, but not awed by the presence of the noted collector in his shop.

"Lady Elizabeth Willoughby does my humble establishment much honor," said he, in perfect English, sweeping his eyes over her without any attempt to conceal his avid interest in her ripe curves. There was a natural arrogance about him, an assurance of power. He had dealt with wealthy white women before, and strange tales were whispered of his dealings with some of them. The air of mystery and power about him made him seem a romantic figure to some European women. "The Bon is in the inner chamber," he said. "There, too, are my real treasures. These," he gestured contemptuously about him, "are only a show for tourists'. If milady would honor me—"

She rose and moved across the room, with the assured bearing of a woman of quality, certain of deference at all time. He drew back a satin curtain on which gilt dragons writhed, and following her through, drew it together behind them. They went along a narrow corridor, where the walls were hung with black velvet and the floor was carpeted with thick Bokhara rugs in which her feet sank deep.

A soft golden glow emanated from bronze lanterns, suspended from the gilt-inlaid ceiling. She felt her pulse quicken. She was on her way to the famous, yet mysterious, inner chamber of Woon Yuen, inaccessible to all but wealthy and beautiful women, and in which, rumor whispered, Woon Yuen had struck strange bargains; He did not always sell his antiques for money, and there were feminine collectors who would barter their virtue for a coveted relic.

Woon Yuen opened a bronze door, worked in gold and ebon inlay, and Arline entered a broad chamber, over a silvery plate of glass set in the threshold. She saw Woon Yuen glance down as she walked over it, and knew he was getting an eyeful. That mirror placed where a woman must walk over it to enter the chamber was a typical Chinese trick to allow the master of the establishment to get a more intimate glimpse of the charms of his fair customers, as reflected in the mirror. She didn't care, but was merely amused at his ingenuity. Even Woon Yuen would hardly dare to make a pass at Lady Elizabeth Willoughby.

He closed the door and bowed her to an ornate mahogany chair.

"Please excuse me for a moment, milady. I will return instantly."

He went out by another door, and she looked about her at a display whose richness might have shamed a shah's treasure-house. Here indeed were the real treasures of Woon Yuen—what looked like the plunder of a thousand sultans' palaces and heathen temples. Idols in jade, gold, and ivory grinned at her, and a less sophisticated woman would have blushed at some of the figures, depicting Oriental gods and goddesses in amorous poses of an astonishing variety. She could imagine the effect these things would have on some of his feminine visitors.

Even her eyes dilated a trifle at the sight of the smirking, pot-bellied monstrosity that was the ivory Bon, looted from God only knew what nameless monastery high in the forbidden Himalayas. Then every nerve tingled as she saw a gold-worked dragon head jutting from the wall beyond the figure. Quickly she turned her gaze back to the god, just as her host returned on silent, velvet-shod feet.

He smiled to see her staring at the idol and the female figure in its arms.

"That is only one of the conceptions of the god—the Tibetan. It is worth, to any collector—but let us delay business talk until after tea. If you will honor me—"

With his guest seated at a small ebon table, the Mongol struck a bronze gong, and tea was served by a slim, silent-footed Chinese girl, clad only in a filmy jacket which came a little below her budding hips, and which concealed none of her smooth-skinned, lemon-tinted charms.

This display, Arline knew, was in accord with the peculiar Chinese belief that a woman is put in a properly receptive mood for amorous advances by the sight of another woman's exposed charms. She wondered, if, after all, Woon Yuen had designs—but he showed no signs of it.

The slave girl bowed herself humbly out with a last salaam that displayed her full breasts beneath the low-necked jacket, and Arline's nerves tightened. Now was the time. She interrupted Woon Yuen's polite trivialities.

"That little jade figure, over there on the ivory shelf," she said, pointing. "Isn't that a piece of Jum Shan's work?"

"I will get it!"

As he rose and stepped to the shelf, she dropped the knock-out pellet into his tea-cup. It dissolved instantly, without discoloring the liquid. She was idly sipping her own tea when the Mongol returned and placed the tiny figure of a jade warrior before her.

"Genuine Jum Shan," said he. "It dates from the tenth century!" He lifted his cup and emptied it at a draught, while she watched him with a tenseness which she could not wholly conceal. He sat the cup down empty, frowning slightly and twitching his lips at the taste.

"I would like to call your attention, milady—" he leaned forward, reaching toward the jade figure—then slumped down across the table, out cold. In an instant she was across the room, and her white, tapering fingers were at work on the teeth of the carved dragon's head. There was an instinct in those fingers, a super-sensitiveness such as skilled cracksmen sometimes have.

In a few moments the jaws gaped suddenly, revealing a velvet-lined nest in the midst of which, like an egg of some fabled bird of paradise, burned and smoldered a great, smooth, round jewel.

She caught her breath as awedly she cupped it in her hands. It was a ruby, of such deep crimson that it looked darkly purple, the hue of old wine, and the blood that flows near the heart. It looked like the materialization of a purple nightmare. She could believe now the wild tales she had heard—that Woon Yuen worshiped it as a god, sucking madness from its sinister depths, that he performed terrible sacrifices to it—

"Lovely, is it not?"

The low voice cracked the tense stillness like the heart-stopping blast of an explosion. She whirled, gasping, then stood transfixed. Woon Yuen stood before her, smiling dangerously, his eyes slits of black fire. A frantic glance sped to the tea-table. There still sprawled a limp, bulky figure, idential to Woon Yuen in every detail.

"What—?" she gasped weakly.

"My shadow," he smiled. "I must be cautious. Long ago I hit upon the expedient of having a servant made up to resemble me, to fool my enemies. When I left the chamber a little while ago, he took my place, and I watched through the peep-hole. I supposed you were after the Heart.

"How did you guess?" She sensed the uselessness of denial.

"Why not? Has not every thief in China tried to steal it?" He spoke softly, but his eyes shone reddishly, and the veins swelled on his neck. "As soon as I learned you were not what you pretended, I knew you had come to steal something. Why not the ruby? I set my trap and let you walk into it. But I must congratulate you on your cleverness. Not one in a thousand could have discovered the way to open the dragon's jaws."

"How did you know I wasn't Lady Elizabeth?" she whispered, dry-lipped; the great ruby seemed to burn her palms.

"I knew it when you walked across the mirror and I saw your lower extremities reflected there, I have never seen Lady Elizabeth, but all dealers in jade know her peculiarities by reputation. One of them is such a passion for jade that she always wears jade-green step-ins. Yours are lavender."

"What are you going to do?" she panted, as he moved toward her.

A light akin to madness burned in his eyes.

"You have defamed the Heart by your touch! It must drink of all who touch it save me, its high priest! If a man, his blood! If a woman—"

No need for him to complete his abominable decree. The ruby fell to the thick carpet, rolled along it like a revolving, demoniac eyeball. She sprang back, shrieking, as Woon Yuen, no longer placid, but with his convulsed face a beast's mask, caught her by the wrist. Against his thickly muscled arms her struggles were vain. As in a nightmare, she felt herself lifted and carried kicking and scratching, through heavily brocaded drapes into a curtained alcove. Her eyes swept the room helplessly; she saw the ivory Bon leering at her as through a mist. It seemed to mock her.

The alcove was walled with mirrors. Only Chinese cruelty could have devised such an arrangement, where, whichever way she twisted her head she was confronted by the spectacle of her own humiliation, reflected from every angle. She was at once actor and spectator in a beastly drama. She could not escape the shameful sight of her own writhings and the eager brutish hands of Woon Yuen remorselessly subduing her hopeless, desperate struggles.

As she felt the greedy yellow fingers on her cringing flesh, she saw in the mirrors, her quivering white breasts, her dress torn—dishevelled, the scarlet skirt in startling contrast to the white thighs, with only a wisp of silk protecting them as they frantically flexed, twisted and writhed—then with a sucking gasp of breath between his grinding teeth, Woon Yuen tore the filmy underthings to rags on her body....

At the tea-table the senseless Chinese still sprawled, deaf to the frantic, agonized shrieks that rang again and again through the inner chamber of Woon Yuen.

An hour later a door opened into a narrow alley in the rear of Woon Yuen's antique shop, and Arline was thrust roughly out, her breasts almost bare, her dress ripped to shreds. She fell sprawling from the force of the shove, and the door was slammed, with a brutal laugh. Dazedly she rose, shook down the remains of her skirt, drew her dress together, and tottered down the alley, sobbing hysterically.

Inside the room from which she had just been ejected, Woon Yuen turned to a lean, saturnine individual, whose pigtail was wound tightly about his head, and from whose wide silk girdle jutted the handle of a light hatchet.

"Yao Chin, take Yun Kang and follow her. There is always some man behind the scenes, when a woman steals. I let her go because I wished her to lead us to that man, send Yun Kang back to me. On no account kill him yourself. I, and only I, must feed the Heart with their vile blood—hers and his."

The hatchetman bowed and left the room, his face showing nothing of his secret belief that Woon Yuen was crazy, not because he believed the Heart drank human blood, but because he, a rich merchant, insisted on doing murder which others of his class always left to hired slayers.

In the mouth of a little twisting alley that ran out upon a rotting abandoned wharf, Arline paused. Her face was haggard and desperate. She had reached the end of her trail. She had failed, and Tremayne would not accept any excuse. Ahead of her she saw only the black muzzles of a firing squad to which he would deliver her—but first there would be torture, inhuman torture, to wring from her secrets her captors would think she possessed. The world at large never knows the full story of the treatment of suspected spies.

With a low moan she covered her eyes with her arm and stumbled blindly toward the edge of the wharf—then a strong arm caught her waist and she looked up into the startled face of Wild Bill Clanton.

"What the hell are you fixin' to do?"

"Let go!" she whimpered. "It's my life! I can end it if I want to!"

"Not with me around," he grunted, picking her up and carrying her back away from the wharf-lip. He sat down on a pile and took her on his lap, like a child. "Good thing I found you," he grunted. "I had a hell of a time tracin' you after you slugged me and ran up that alley, but I finally saw you duckin' down this one. You pick the damndest places to stroll in. Now you tell me what the trouble is. A classy dame like you don't need to go jumpin' off of docks."

He seemed to hold no grudge for that clout with the pitcher. There was possessiveness in the clasp of his arms about her supple body, but she found a comforting solidity in the breast muscles against which her flaxen head rested. There was a promise of security in his masculine strength. Suddenly she no longer resented his persistent pursuit of her. She needed his strength—needed a man who would fight for her.

In a few words she told him everything—the hold Tremayne had on her, the task he had set for her, and what had happened in Woon Yuen's inner room.

He swore at the narrative.

"Ill get that yellow-belly for that! But first we'll go to the Alley of Rats. Try to stall Tremayne along to give you another chance. In the meantime I'll work on a Eurasian wench I know who could tell me plenty about him—and she will, too, or I'll skin her alive. He's been mixed up in plenty of crooked rackets. If we get somethin' hot on him, we can shut his mouth, all right. And we'll get somethin', you can bet."

When they entered the Alley of Rats, in a half-abandoned warehouse district in the native quarter, they did not see two furtive figures slinking after them, nor hear the taller whisper: "Yun Kang, go back and tell our master she had led us to a man! I will watch the alley till he comes."

Clanton and Arline turned into a dingy doorway, and went down a corridor that seemed wholly deserted. Groping along it, in the dusk, she found the room she sought and led Clanton into it. She lit a candle stub stuck on a shelf, and turned to Clanton: "He'll be here soon."

"I'll wait in the next room," he said, reluctantly taking his arm from about her waist. "If he gets rough, I'll come in."

Alone in the candle-lighted room she tried to compose herself; her heart was beating a wild tattoo, loud in the stillness. Somewhere rats scampered noisily. Time dragged insufferably. Then quick, light steps sounded in the hall, and Duke Tremayne burst through the door, his eyes blazing with greed. They turned red as he read defeat in her eyes; his face contorted.

"Damn you!" His fingers were like talons as he gripped her shoulders. "You failed!"

"I couldn't help it!" she pleaded. "He knew I was a fake. Please don't hurt me, Duke. I'll try again—"

"Try again? You little fool! Do you think that Chinese devil will give you another chance?" Tremayne's suavity was gone; he was like a madman. "You failed, after all my planning! All right! I'll have a little profit out of you! Take off that dress—" Already in shreds, the garment ripped easily in his grasp, baring a white breast which quivered under his gaze.

24

The inner door swung open. Tremayne wheeled, drawing a pistol, but before he could fire, Clanton's fist crashed against his jaw and stretched him senseless. Clanton bent and picked up the gun, then whirled as the hall door opened behind him. He stiffened as a tranquil voice spoke: "Do not move, my friend!"

He looked into the muzzle of a gun in Woon Yuen's hand.

"So you are the man?" muttered the Mongol. "Good! The Heart drinks—"

He could fire before Clanton could lift the pistol he held. But behind the American Arline laughed suddenly, unexpectedly.

"It worked, Bill!" she exclaimed. "Our man will get the ruby while we hold Woon Yuen here! The fool! He hasn't yet guessed that we tricked him to draw him away from his shop after I'd found where he hid the gem."

Woon Yuen's face went ashen. With a choking cry he fired, not at Clanton but at the girl. But his hand was shaking like a leaf. He missed, and like an echo of his shot came the crack of Clanton's pistol. Woon Yuen dropped, drilled through the head.

"Good work, kid!" Clanton cried exultantly. "He fell for it—hard!"

"But they'll hang us for this!" whimpered the girl. "Listen! Someone's running up the hall! They've heard the shots!"

Stooping swiftly Clanton folded Duke Tremayne's fingers about the butt of the smoking pistol, and then kicked the man heavily in the shins. Tremayne grunted and showed signs of returning consciousness. Clanton drew Arline into the other room and they watched through the crack of the door.

The hall door opened and Yao Chin came in like a panther, hatchet in hand. His eyes blazed at the sight of Woon Yuen on the floor, Tremayne staggering to his feet, a pistol in his hand. With one stride the hatchetman reached the reeling blackmailer. There was a flash of steel, an ugly butcher-shop crunch, and Tremayne slumped, his skull split. Yao Chin tossed the reeking hatchet to the floor beside his victim and turned away.

"Out of here, quick!" muttered Clanton, shaking Arline who seemed threatened with hysteria. "Up the alley—in the other direction."

She regained her poise in their groping flight up the darkened alley, as Clanton muttered: "We're in the clear now. Tremayne can't talk, with his head split, and that hatchetman'll tell his pals Tremayne shot their boss."

"We'd better get out of town!" They had emerged into a narrow, lamp-lit street.

"Why? We're safe from suspicion now." A little tingle of pleasure ran through her as Clanton turned into a doorway and spoke to a grinning old Chinaman who bowed them into a small neat room, with curtained windows and a couch.

As the door closed behind the old Chinese, Clanton caught her hungrily to him, finding her red lips, now unresisting. Her arms went about his thick neck as he lifted her bodily from the floor. Willingly she yielded, responded to his eager caresses.

She had only exchanged masters, it was true, but this was different. There was a delicious sense of comfort and security in a strong man who could fight for her and protect her. There was pleasure in the dominance of his strong hands. With a blissful sigh she settled herself luxuriously in his powerful arms.